HE SAVES the DAY

To Nate and Marc,
who always save my day —M. H.

For Paco —L. C.

He Saves the Day

Marsha Hayles • ILLUSTRATED BY Lynne Cravath

G. P. PUTNAM'S SONS • NEW YORK

Library of Congress Cataloging-in-Publication Data
Hayles, Marsha.   He saves the day / Marsha Hayles; illustrated by Lynne Cravath.   p.   cm.   Summary: In a plane or race car, on the high seas, in a jungle or before a castle, a brave and daring champion saves the day, but sometimes he needs help. [1. Heroes—Fiction. 2. Stories in rhyme.] I. Cravath, Lynne Woodcock, ill. II. Title. PZ8.3.H32He 2001 [E]—dc21 99-20713
ISBN 0-399-23363-6   10 9 8 7 6 5 4 3 2 1
First Impression

From his runway,
He takes off and flies.

He swoops, he soars,
He tips the sky.

His engines fail.
"Oh, no!" he cries.
A spiraling spin,
It's do or die.

With wing flaps down
And spirits high,

HE SAVES THE DAY!

Again he flies!

On his racecourse,
He sets the pace.

He vrooms, he zooms,
One speedy ace.

A dangerous curve,
The worst he's faced.

He skids, he swerves,
There goes first place!

He hits the gas,
Speeds off in haste.

HE
SAVES
THE
DAY!

And wins the race!

Atop his ship,
He sails the seas.
He rides the waves,
He tames the breeze.

"Look! Up ahead,
What can that be?
A pirate ship,
Attacking me!"

His cannons flash,
Those villains flee.

HE SAVES
THE DAY!

Such bravery!

In his jungle,
He's one brave guide.

Adventure calls
From every side.

When suddenly,
Fierce tiger eyes

Glare down at him,
Great jaws spread wide.

He leaps and swings,
On vines he rides.

HE SAVES THE DAY!

Away he glides!

At his castle,
He rides by all.
His armor bright,
His horse so tall.

He wields his sword
When battle calls.

He leaps, he strikes—
OH, NO! He falls!

His lady brave
Breaks up the brawl.

SHE SAVES THE DAY!

He can't save
them all!